For Puma, who gave me wings.

And thank you to Emma Ledbetter, Ann Bobco,
Reka Simonsen, and Sonia Chaghatzbanian.

when you
need wings
lita judge

Atheneum Books for Young Readers

New York London Toronto
Sydney New Delhi

On a day when you feel
like no one is listening,

and everyone is **LOUD**,

and you are afraid,

and you wish you could just disappear,

Little
Dreamers
Preschool

shut your eyes and listen.

Do you hear it?

That isn't your heart.

That is the sound of your very own wings,

beating within.

They can't be seen by others,

but you can hear them and feel them

and use them . . . to fly far away,

if you need to today,

to find treasures

that live inside
your mind.

To laugh

and dance

and find bravehearted friends.

To go a little wild

and even to

ROAR!

So, listen closely.

Do you hear it?

That is the sound of
your wings,

giving you strength

to fly.

ATHENEUM
BOOKS FOR
YOUNG READERS

An imprint of Simon & Schuster Children's Publishing Division
1230 Avenue of the Americas, New York, New York 10020
Copyright © 2020 by Lita Judge • All rights reserved, including the right of
reproduction in whole or in part in any form. • ATHENEUM BOOKS FOR
YOUNG READERS is a registered trademark of Simon & Schuster, Inc.
Atheneum logo is a trademark of Simon & Schuster, Inc.
For information about special discounts for bulk purchases, please contact
Simon & Schuster Special Sales at 1-866-506-1949 or business@simonandschuster.com.
The Simon & Schuster Speakers Bureau can bring authors to your live event.
For more information or to book an event, contact the Simon & Schuster Speakers Bureau
at 1-866-248-3049 or visit our website at www.simonspeakers.com.
Jacket design by Sonia Chaghatzbanian and Karyn Lee • Interior design by Karyn Lee
The text for this book was set in Adobe Caslon Pro. • The illustrations for this book were rendered
in pencil and watercolor. • Manufactured in China • 1219 SCP • First Edition
2 4 6 8 10 9 7 5 3 1
Library of Congress Cataloging-in-Publication Data • Names: Judge, Lita, author, illustrator. •
Title: When you need wings / by Lita Judge. • Description: First edition. | New York : Atheneum,
[2020] • Summary: Illustrations and easy-to-read text advise the reader to seek self-confidence
on the wings of imagination. • Identifiers: LCCN 2018046691 | ISBN 9781534437555
(hardcover) | ISBN 9781534437548 (eBook) • Subjects: | CYAC: Self-
confidence—Fiction. | Imagination—Fiction.• Classification:
LCC PZ7.J894 Wh 2020| DDC [E]—dc23 • LC record available
at https://lccn.loc.gov/2018046691